Olaf Loves . . . Everything!

By Andrea Posner-Sanchez
Illustrated by the Disney Storybook Art Team

A Random House PICTUREBACK® Book
Random House 🏠 New York

Copyright © 2016 Disney Enterprises, Inc. All rights reserved. Published in the United States by Random House
Children's Books, a division of Penguin Random House LLC, 1745 Broadway, New York, NY 10019, and in
Canada by Penguin Random House Canada Limited, Toronto, in conjunction with Disney Enterprises, Inc. Pictureback,
Random House, and the Random House colophon are registered trademarks of Penguin Random House LLC.
randomhousekids.com
ISBN 978-0-7364-3590-1
Printed in the United States of America
10 9 8 7 6 5 4 3 2 1

Olaf loves so many things. He loves flowers. "Mmm, this flower smells soooo sweet!"

"Look, Anna! Look, Elsa!" Olaf cries.
"A heart-shaped flower petal. Isn't it wonderful?"

Olaf loves bumblebees.
"Hello, fuzzy little guy!" he says.

Olaf even loves chasing bumblebees.
"Oooh, you're a fast flier!" he says, happily
running after the bee.

Olaf loves dancing . . .

. . . especially with seagulls!
"Now for the big finish!"
Olaf twirls on one foot.

Olaf loves picnics.
"Eating outside is so much fun!" he tells his friends.

Olaf even loves rainy picnics.
"This is the greatest day!" he cheers.

Olaf loves making sand angels . . .

...and sand sculptures. Who do you think
these two look like?

Olaf loves hearts. Anna finds
a heart-shaped leaf.
"Oooh, that's the prettiest
leaf I've ever seen!"

Anna and Kristoff trim a hedge into
the shape of a heart for their snowy friend.
"I love it!" Olaf exclaims.

"Don't move, Sven!" Olaf cries. "I just *looove* butterflies! Especially when they look like hearts!"

Olaf loves all his friends.

And Olaf loves *you*!